D0592822

3/14

FAIRY TALE COLLECTION

The LITTLE MERMAID

RETOLD BY REBECCA FELIX
ILLUSTRATED BY KATHLEEN PETELINSEK

Published by The Child's World®
1980 Lookout Drive • Mankato, MN 56003-1705
800-599-READ • www.childsworld.com

Acknowledgments
The Child's World®: Mary Berendes, Publishing Director
Red Line Editorial: Editorial direction
The Design Lab: Design, production, and illustration

Copyright © 2014 by Peterson Publishing Company. All rights reserved.
No part of this book may be reproduced or utilized in any form or by
any means without written permission from the publisher.

ISBN 978-1623236120
LCCN 2013931333

Printed in the United States of America
Mankato, MN
July, 2013
PA02179

F ar, far from shore are the deepest, bluest waters of the sea. At the bottom of these waters once lived the people of the sea. These mermaids and mermen had fishtails where human legs would be. A widowed king of the sea ruled. He lived in a swirling castle of coral and shells with his mother and six daughters.

The six sea princesses were beauties. Each had a voice more lovely than the last. The littlest mermaid's voice was more beautiful than any sound ever heard above the sea and across the land. But the little mermaid was often quiet.

She would get lost in daydreams about the human world. Her grandmother often told great tales of the land and its people, adding to her imagination.

Upon turning fifteen, each sea princess would be allowed to rise and explore the sea's surface and shore. After each sister turned fifteen, she returned from the surface with dazzling descriptions. There were twinkling stars and city lights. Tall forests lined the shore. And humans sailed great ships with fluttering sails.

Finally, the little mermaid's fifteenth birthday arrived. She reached the surface just before sunset. The sun's rays lit up the sky and shone over the ocean surface. The little mermaid blinked in delight.

She saw a huge ship in the distance. She swam close and looked in a porthole. She saw people with two legs. She knew they must be humans. She spotted a handsome young prince at the center of a jolly gathering. The little mermaid fell in love with him at once.

Suddenly the little mermaid felt the sea shift. A quiet sunset turned into a violent storm. Whitecaps rose toward blackened skies. The ship split in two.

The humans were flushed underwater. The little mermaid knew humans could not breathe under the water. She dove for the prince. She reached him just as his eyes closed. She brought him to the surface. There they floated all night.

By morning, they reached shore. The prince's eyes remained closed. The little mermaid placed him on the sand. Just then, loud bells rang out. People spilled from a steepled building on the beach.

The little mermaid quickly returned to the waves. She watched the people from behind a sea stack. She saw a human girl spot the prince. The girl ran to him, calling to the crowd for help.

The noise woke the prince. His eyes met the girl's. He grabbed her hand. But the crowd pressed in and carried him away. The little mermaid's heart dropped to the bottom of the sea. The prince would never know of the little mermaid who saved his life.

The little mermaid went to her grandmother in despair. "I want to be human!" she cried.

"But why? Mermaid lives are 300 years long. Human's lives are much shorter," said her grandmother.

This only made the little mermaid sob. "I have fallen in love with a human prince," she choked.

"Well . . . human lives are short, but they do have souls that live on forever," said the grandmother to comfort her granddaughter.

This made the little mermaid wish even more to become human. Mermaids did not have souls. They dissolved into sea foam upon dying. The little mermaid decided to visit the evil witch of the sea for advice.

"I already know what brings you to me!" the sea witch shouted as the little mermaid

entered her lair. "It is foolish. But I will grant your wish—with sacrifice and due price."

A potion would transform the little mermaid's fishtail to legs so she could live on land. If the prince loved her more than any other and married her, she would gain a human soul.

But—the little mermaid would never live as a mermaid again. And if the prince married another? She would immediately die a mermaid's death, becoming sea foam.

"And these are just the terms!" laughed the sea witch. "There are also two prices to pay."

The first was pain. Each step on human feet would feel as though the little mermaid walked on fire or knives. The little mermaid would also have to give her lovely voice to the sea witch. She would never speak or sing again.

The little mermaid shut her eyes tight. She thought of a soul. She thought of the prince. Her tears disappeared into the sea as she agreed.

The next morning, the little mermaid awoke on the shore of the prince's castle. She looked down and saw two legs in place of her fishtail.

She looked up and saw . . . the prince! He asked who she was, but she could not answer.

The prince took the little mermaid to his castle. The two became fast friends even though the little mermaid couldn't speak. But, oh, the things the prince spoke to *her* about!

He spoke of his love for a human girl who had once rescued him on the beach. He had searched for her ever since. This hurt the little mermaid. If only she could tell the prince it was *she* who had saved him! She hoped he would never find the girl from the beach.

But find her he did. And the day they were reunited, the prince declared he would marry the human girl from the beach the very next morning.

The heartbroken little mermaid stared out over the sea that night. Suddenly, her five sisters appeared in the waves. They were bald! They had learned of her deal with the sea witch. And they traded to the witch all their beautiful hair for a chance to save their sister.

They gave the little mermaid a knife. She was to take the prince's life with it before the morning. For his death, the sea witch would restore her fishtail and life as a mermaid, but not her voice.

But the little mermaid couldn't bring herself to hurt the prince. She threw the knife into the ocean and dove in after it.

She waited to fade to foam. Through the night, the little mermaid felt herself dissolving and changing form. But as the morning sun

rose, she felt herself rising with it. She was floating. And she felt alive!

The little mermaid looked around. She saw transparent people among the clouds. "We are people of the air," one whispered.

"We float for 300 years, doing good deeds in order to earn souls," breathed another. "You are now one of us."

The little mermaid smiled. She had been given the chance to earn a soul. And she regained her voice. It rang in song as she floated as high as the sea is deep.

FAIRY TALES

The story of the little mermaid is a very old tale. It was first written by Hans Christian Andersen and published in 1837. Andersen lived in Denmark and wrote many stories that became classic fairy tales. These include "The Princess and the Pea," "The Ugly Duckling," and "The Emperor's New Clothes." Throughout the years, many people have retold Andersen's tales, including "The Little Mermaid." While this retelling remains close to the original story, some have new twists and turns. The Disney Company wrote one version and turned it into a popular animated film in 1989. In that version, the little mermaid wins back her voice *and* the heart of the prince at the end! If you were retelling the story, what twists would you add? Would you change the ending?

The story of the little mermaid is fun to tell, especially because it takes place in a mysterious world under the sea. But similar to most fairy tales, the story also makes us think and maybe even teaches us a lesson. The little mermaid was not happy being a mermaid. She wanted to become human and explore another world. To do this, she gave up and lost many important things. Do you think the little mermaid thought the sacrifices she made were worth it in the end? Do you think they were?

ABOUT THE AUTHOR

Rebecca Felix is a writer and editor. She lives in Florida, near the sea. She grew up reading classic fairy tales and loves working on children's books today.

ABOUT THE ILLUSTRATOR

Kathleen Petelinsek loves to draw and paint. She lives next to a lake in southern Minnesota with her husband, Dale; two daughters, Leah and Anna; two dogs, Gary and Rex; and her fluffy cat, Emma.